Bittersweet Chocolate
By: C.M. Guidroz

Also by C.M. Guidroz

Bite-Sized Rage

A Shotgun House in N'awlins

My Sweet Livy

Play Me a Song

It's Me Charlie

Love and Formaldehyde

All I Want for Christmas is You

A Crack in the Foundation

This book is dedicated to the extraordinary readers who willingly journey into the shadows with me, embracing the dark and twisted stories I create. Thank you.

Trigger Warnings:

Infidelity
Domestic violence
Emotional violence
Blood
Torture
Murder
Sexual content
Body Mutilation

Content Warning: This book contains mature themes, explicit content, and explores sensitive topics that may be triggering to some readers. It is intended for individuals aged 18 and over. The narrative delves into psychological and emotional complexities, addressing themes such as mental health, explicit violence, and sexual content. Reader discretion is advised, and it is recommended for those who are comfortable engaging with intense and dark subject matter.

If you are sensitive to any of these themes, please consider your own well-being before proceeding.

In this book, all characters, events, and locations are purely fictional. Any resemblance to actual persons, living or dead, or events is coincidental and not intended. The author's imagination has crafted the narrative, and any similarities to real-life situations or individuals are entirely unintentional. This work is a product of creativity, and any perceived connections to the real world are purely coincidental.

Prologue

In the quiet corridors of suburbia, where manicured lawns whispered tales of ordinary lives, I stood on the precipice of my own unraveling. Our house, a carefully curated sanctuary of domestic bliss, hid the storms brewing within its walls—the storms that gave no warning, the flip of a switch, the great awakening. Whatever you want to call it, it doesn't matter. Looking out from the back porch at the new garden, I feel a sense of pride and relief.

Although, they will say I lost it. The pressures of motherhood weigh down on a new mother. I always thought that was a funny thing to say. "She's lost it," and lost what exactly? My mind? No, that can't be it because nothing has been more clear to me than right now. No, I haven't lost anything; I have found exactly what I have been looking for—myself.

My cheeks feel tight against the morning breeze as I stand on the back porch. Confused, I touch my fingers to them. Am I crying? Are these tears of happiness or regret? Pulling my fingers away, I see the crimson tips, and I'm reminded that it's just blood. So much blood. I'll have to jump in the shower before the sitter drops off Jake.

The heart-shaped box in my hands offers me one more chocolate. So with blood-stained fingers, I eat the small square from the Valentine's Day heart I bought myself. This will be a Valentine's Day I'll never forget.

Closing the box of chocolates, I read the cover. Flowers in bright colors surround the words, "My love blooms for you." And I really do lose it. A fit of giggles takes over me. I look back at the garden and wonder if anything will bloom from the shit I buried here.

Chapter One

Jake's rhythmic breathing beside me was a comforting backdrop to my thoughts as I sat cross-legged in bed, contemplating the prospect of diving back into the world of books. I hadn't even moved him to his "big boy bed" yet before I started pulling books off my shelf. The bedside table held a stack of unread novels – the casualties of my fleeting resolutions to read more. Every year, the pile grew taller, a silent testament to my aspirations thwarted by the daily demands of motherhood. Jake was a fussy baby and took a lot of attention. He still does, but now at three years old, he's a little more independent.

But today, a newfound determination simmered within me, fueled by the thought of exploring the literary haven that was "Booktok." I had stumbled across a woman's TikTok, and she was talking about a book with such excitement; it was contagious. I wanted to feel passionate about something. With my phone in hand, I navigated through the app, following everyone who held up a book in the first few seconds of their video.

A sense of excitement simmered under my skin, envisioning myself scrolling through endless book recommendations, engaging in passionate discussions about fictional worlds, and perhaps even finding other humans to talk to that aren't asking for snacks or pissing on my floor. Potty training is a bitch. The allure of Booktok seemed irresistible, and I couldn't help but smile at the prospect of discovering new stories while Jake napped. The idea that I could make friends with similar people, and have some sense of community, was exciting to me. Maybe I'm just desperate. Maybe this is another cry for help disguised as a hobby. I just can't remember the times before when I wasn't just a stay-at-home mom.

Don't get me wrong I love my son, and I love being a mother. I would love it even more if I didn't feel so alone while doing it.

The "mom groups" aren't for me. I know the dynamic of social groups like that. All smiles and support till you admit that you shoved the tablet in your son's face so you didn't have to sit on the floor bashing toy cars with him for the 100th time. Smiles hide the judgments, and gossip is disguised as support. So it's just me and Jake till Mark gets home. Lately, it feels like he's never home though.

The door creaked open, and Mark entered, a cloud of discontent trailing behind him like an unwelcome shadow. He sees Jake in the bed and gives me the look. He's fresh out of the shower and ready to lay in bed, Jake taking up his spot.

"What are you up to now, Emily?" Mark's voice carried a tone of irritation as if the mere act of sitting in bed with my phone had disrupted the delicate balance of the universe. He looks past me at the stack of books

.

I looked up, optimism still shimmering in my eyes. "Hey, I was just thinking about joining Booktok. You know, for reading recommendations and stuff. It sounds like fun, and I can do it during Jake's naps." I say, whether I was ignoring his attitude or used to it I can't say.

Mark's response was an exasperated sigh as if the very idea of me adopting another hobby was an inconvenience he couldn't bear. "Another hobby? How much money will this cost me this time?" His words were sharp, a disdainful sneer accompanying each syllable.

I felt a pang of disappointment, my enthusiasm deflating like a balloon struck by an unseen arrow. "I already have a ton of books I can read, other than a few books here and there it shouldn't cost a lot and I thought it could be a nice way to connect with other readers. You know, during those moments when Jake is sleeping."

Mark's eyes narrowed, a condescending smirk playing on his lips. "Connect with other readers? Is that code for spending more time on your phone instead of doing something productive?"

I bit my lip, resisting the urge to unleash a torrent of frustration. Instead, I took a deep breath, trying to salvage the remnants of my excitement. "It's just a way to enjoy reading again, Mark. You don't have to act like such an ass."

His response was a dismissive wave as he headed towards the door. "Just don't let it turn into another one of your fleeting hobbies, Emily. I mean when are you going to stick with one thing? You hop from hobby to hobby and I'm the one who has to fork out the money for it. Get Jake to his bed I'm ready to lay down."

The door clicked shut, leaving me alone with the fading echoes of his disapproval. The fact that he's not entirely wrong only makes his words sting more. I have taken on many hobbies over the years but I am trying to find myself. How will I know what I enjoy if I don't try new things? The sense of excitement I feel when I start a new hobby is more than Mark has given me in months. I discover a hobby that piques my interest, then I research it endlessly and make lists of everything I need. Riding the high of a new hobby is great until you start to come down and lose interest. Then I'm on to the next hobby, chasing the high of feeling something, anything.

The room felt suddenly smaller, the weight of unspoken expectations pressing down on my shoulders. Putting my phone down, I slowly pick Jake up and carry him to his room. I place a small kiss on his forehead before I creep out of his room, hearing the bed adjust to Mark's weight. I know he is already in bed, phone in hand. He will scroll until he finally turns over to tell me goodnight.

I steady my thoughts and try to wipe the disappointment off my face as I make my way across the room to my side of the bed. The tension between us was lingering like a heavy mist. The rhythmic hum of the ceiling fan seemed to underscore the unspoken words hanging in the air. I turned towards Mark, searching for a connection amid the growing chasm between us.

"Mark, I really need your support. This is just a small thing for me, a way to reconnect with something I love. I used to read all the time."

He glanced up from his phone with narrowed eyes, as if asking him not to be a jerk was too much of a request. "Support? Emily, I'm the one paying for everything. Isn't that support enough?"

His words stung, an insinuation that financial contributions equated to emotional support. I took a deep breath, trying to maintain my composure. "It's not just about money, Mark. I need you to be there for me, to understand my need for something to be passionate about."

A self-assured smirk played on Mark's lips. "Something to be passionate about? We have a child, Emily. Motherhood should be enough for you."

The condescension in his voice had my blood boiling under my skin. "Being a mother is incredible, but I'm more than just that. I need something for myself, too. I told you I already have books to read; I don't need money. I was just trying to talk to you. But whatever." I try to keep my voice down to not wake Jake, but he's not usually this outspoken and mean. The past few months have been a complete change in temperature with him.

Mark rubs his face with both hands, exhaling frustration before turning to me. "You're lucky I provide for you, Em. I am giving you a gift that some women would actually be grateful for. Some women would kill to be in your position. You get to stay home all day with Jake; I never asked you to go back to work. I know motherhood is a full-time job, and honestly, I don't think you could handle anything more. I wasn't trying to be unsupportive; I was just trying to remind you that you have more important things to worry about than going through hobby after fucking hobby, wasting our money."

"That's not fair, Mark. I love being a mother, but I'm allowed to have other interests. I can't believe we are even fighting over this. I just wanted to talk to you." The fight in me deflates with a sigh. I can feel him looking at me, but I can't even meet his eyes. I don't know what changed between us, but on nights like tonight, I feel the changes squeeze my heart a little harder.

"Now I'm the bad guy again. I can't win with you, Em. Come on, don't be mad at me for being honest with you. I love you. Let's not argue before bed." Mark says, reaching over to touch my knee, and I never noticed how foreign his touch feels now.

"It's fine," I whispered, a weary acceptance settling over me. "Let's just go to sleep."
Mark removes his hand, and I miss his warmth instantly, even if it was just an attempt to stop this argument. We fall right back into routine; he shuts off the light, turns over, and resumes scrolling on his phone while I'm left feeling alone. As I lay in the dark, staring at the ceiling, I couldn't help but wonder if this was the compromise I had unwittingly signed up for – a life where dreams were sacrificed on the altar of financial stability. The echoes of Mark's words reverberated in my mind, and I questioned whether my pursuit of individuality would always be met with resistance.

Closing my eyes, I allowed the night to swallow me whole.

Chapter Two

The morning sunlight spilled through the kitchen window, casting a warm hue over the countertops. As I moved through the familiar motions of preparing breakfast for Jake, I couldn't shake the lingering echoes of the previous night's conversation with Mark. The weight of his disapproval still clung to my thoughts like a stubborn shadow. Jake smiles at me as I hand him his breakfast, and the weight of my emotions eases up a little. As he eats, my eyes unfocus, and my mind drifts back to last night.

I replay the fight with Mark in my head like a movie. I watch as he barks from his side of the bed while my hand slowly reaches for the stack of books. The version of myself in my mind stares blankly forward in my direction as if I'm standing in the doorway of our bedroom. A witness to what is about to happen. The version of myself locks eyes with me before a sinister smile creeps across her face. It happens so fast—I watch as she grabs a book from the stack and slams it across Mark's face. His barking stops as his head bounces off the headboard with a sickening crack. She jumps on top of him and slams the book down over and over again, blood spattering the headboard. I watch in silent amazement as she stands up, covered in Mark's blood, and looks right at me. Mark's feet twitch at the end of the bed as he continues to make weak gargled sounds. She points at my hands hanging at my side. When I look at them, they are covered in blood.

"Oh-oh, Mommy." Jake's voice slams me back into reality and out of whatever daydream that was. My hands are wet with spilled milk as they rest on the table. I shake off the hazy feeling as I smile at Jake and clean the mess he made while I was lost in my thoughts.

After breakfast and a whirlwind of morning activities with Jake, the moment arrived when his drooping eyes signaled that it was nap time. As I laid him down for his afternoon slumber, I tiptoed out of his room, my thoughts drawn to the stack of untouched books on the bedside table. The books, once a source of excitement, now seemed to mock me with their untouched spines and unexplored worlds. Doubt gnawed at the edges of my determination. Was it selfish to want more than the routine of motherhood? I mean, it's just a book. Mark's words echoed, questioning my pursuits beyond the domestic sphere. My mind flashes back to his head bouncing off the headboard, and I surprise myself when my mouth quirks up a bit in a smile.

Despite the internal conflict, I picked up a book from the stack and made my way to the living room. The weight of the book in my hands felt reassuring, a tangible connection to a world beyond my daily routine. I stand in the living room and swing the book with both hands, testing the weight, to see if I was capable of doing what the dream version of me did. What am I doing? Shaking my head, I settled into the couch and opened the book.

As the first chapter unfolded before me, time seemed to slip through my fingers like grains of sand. Before I knew it, Jake came wobbling into the living room, and two hours had passed. As he crawls on the couch next to me, I close the book, bookmarking the page with a mix of disappointment and reluctance.

"Good nap, bud?" I ask as he cuddles on my lap, still rubbing his eyes. Then he pops up and hops off the couch.

"Yep, you play." He says as he dumps the bucket of toy cars, and I join him on the floor. The afternoon unfolded in a game of tag outside, followed by more toy car races and cleaning up before I had to start dinner. Jake sits on the couch with a cheese stick in his hand while the little blue dog bounces across the screen of the TV. He will be occupied for a whole fifteen minutes, maybe. My phone rings, vibrating the counter until I pick it up. Mark's voice sounds distant and quiet, as he tells me he won't be home till later due to another night at the office. I feigned disappointment, a skill I'd honed to perfection, but beneath the surface, a quiet relief lingered. A night free from the weight of his condescension and the suffocating atmosphere of our unraveling marriage.

As I hung up the phone, a strange mix of emotions enveloped me. Part of me longed for the days when his presence brought comfort, but lately, every interaction felt like navigating a minefield of tension. Our marriage, once filled with passion and excitement, underwent a shift after Jake came along. The guilt of such thoughts about my son's arrival weighs heavily on me as I watch him smile at the TV. The truth is laid out in front of me and it doesn't care how I feel about it. I'm alone and I've been alone for a long time. Before Jake, Mark was attentive and sweet. My need for a hobby wasn't as strong, I'll admit, but the need was still there. I have a "she-shed" in the backyard to prove it. I used it when I was trying out pottery. Mark would come in just to watch and talk about his day. We never had the iconic ghost moment, him molding the clay from behind me. We did however break a bowl when he fucked me on one of the tables I have in there. A smile crosses my face at the memory of when he touched me with hands that didn't feel heavy with judgment.

    After Jake, Mark started working more leaving me alone to do my duties as a mother. The duties he reminds me of daily with his sighs of disappointment when things aren't perfect. The amount of days he doesn't touch me adds up to him no longer being attracted to my post-pregnancy body. The hands that used to set my skin on fire are now frozen solid with the weight of my insecurities. After Jake, I realized I was alone.

We moved away from home for Mark's job so I don't have a mother-in-law who gives unsolicited parenting advice or a mother who hovers over my shoulder. My mother wouldn't be much help anyway. I still have the scars from her failure as a mother. The pressure to be a better mom than her lingers in my thoughts almost daily. The memories of my childhood are in a box I don't want to open, scared of the monsters it may unleash.

Moving on autopilot I fall back into the nightly routine of cleaning up and getting Jake to bed. With Jake tucked in, I tiptoed into the hall stopping abruptly when I saw a small red dot on the floor. Looking up I see the trail of red spots leading to our bedroom. I bend down the investigate what Jake or myself could have spilled. A cold chill sweeps over me when I pinch the sticky thick fluid in between my fingers, this is blood. Following the trail to the slightly open door of Mark and I's bedroom I remember my bloody hands from my daydream this morning. Pushing open the door my breath stops completely at the scene before me. She's here again, except she is me and she is standing in front of my bed swinging a red rope of tissue around her neck like a scarf. The tubular length of whatever that is is wet with blood as she swings the end at me, like some enticing dancer. Looking past her I see Mark's body and the bile rises and burns my throat. His eyes distant and cloudy stare at me, his foot no longer twitching because he is gone this time.

She, who is me, walks over to the side of the bed, and to my stunned amazement, I follow her. She laughs but there is no sound except for the ringing in my ears, my pulse beating like a drum. She climbs on top of his body, straddling him, his chest and stomach open and wet with gore. Throwing her head back she starts to bounce up and down on him, swinging what I now know is his intestines around like she's on some wild bull. I stare as the tissue and sinew drop to the floor with each bounce, her mouth forming silent moans of pleasure as she rubs the organ still wrapped around her throat all over her body. A metallic smell enters my nose and a copper taste fills my mouth.

    I blink hard again trying to get rid of the scene playing out before me but it doesn't work. All I can do is watch, back pressed against the blood-splattered wall as a sick version of me rides the corpse of my husband. Unraveling the fleshy rope from her neck she then leans back, lifting her bloodied nightgown to expose herself, legs spread wide. That's when she turns her head and locks eyes with me again, smiling that sinister smile as she slowly packs the soft meat between the bloody lips of her cunt. Head thrown back, she packs more and more of the intestines into her body as I watch, a voyeur to my insanity. When she looks back at me, legs spread wide, the meaty rope hanging out of her like a fucked up umbilical cord, she smiles and uses her other hand to work her clit. Watching in stunned silence I can't take my eyes off of her. My eyes are wide with shock, I watch as her body starts to twitch and shake with her release, and for a moment I'm envious of her pleasure. She looks at me, blinking slowly with eyes that are heavy with release, as she stands up from the bed.

She walks toward me, the bloodied mess of an organ trailing behind her, and stops inches in front of my face. The expression on her face is soft even though it is coated in blood. She looks from my eyes to my lips and I feel her gore-covered hand slide up the side of my neck. I shock myself as I lean into it, the longing to be caressed in this way overwhelming me. When her wet, crimson lips touch mine I feel a jolt of electricity as I close my eyes and fall into her kiss. When I open my eyes, I shudder as breath fills my lungs again, like I'd been holding it this whole time.

The room was clean and bright, with not a single drop of blood in sight. My fingertips graze my lips and as I move off of the wall I am aware of two things. The fact that I am losing my mind but more importantly, I'm aware of my arousal coating my thighs.

Chapter Three

I miss her.

Why hasn't she been back?

Why am I like this?

Weeks passed like a blur since the daydreams first whispered their tantalizing secrets into the recesses of my mind. In the quiet moments, their echoes lingered, teasing the edges of my consciousness. Luckily, with Jake, there weren't many quiet moments. Still, I found myself yearning for the version of myself that existed in those forbidden fantasies – a woman unburdened by guilt, open in her desires, and unrestrained in the pursuit of affection.

As I moved through the mundane motions of the days, the longing for that liberated version of myself grew like a quiet storm. The ache for a touch, *her touch*, was almost unbearable.

What is happening to me?

I have been reading books but the words stay on the page, never making it through the barrier of my thoughts. This is usually when I would drop this whole book hobby and move on to something else that gives me the sense of fulfillment I'm searching for. Except, I have a new obsession and it's her.

No, stop.

It's not her, it's the pursuit of my own pleasure from my husband, the need to fix whatever seems to be broken. I couldn't help but wonder if our story had reached its final chapter, or if there was still a chance to rewrite the narrative and rediscover the love that had been lost in the shadows. The days have passed in a haze but today something seems clearer. The fog lifting enough to see that I can fix this.

When Mark texted to say he would be working late again, I felt my motivation start to deflate. How can I fix us if he is never home anymore? I have to fix us or she will be back, and while I have longed for her kiss to touch my lips again I know it's not right. I know that she is my insanity molded into the form of the me I want to be, and giving myself to her is giving myself over to the trenches of my madness. I'm trapped in a sick love triangle with my husband and my insanity.

I grab my phone, the weight of the yearning becoming too much to bear. I dial the number of a sitter we rarely use, crafting a delicate plan to steal a few precious hours away. Jake would be in capable hands, and I could surprise Mark with dinner at the office. I used to surprise him with lunch at work, stolen kisses on company time before the task became too tedious balancing a car seat in one hand and a bag of food in another. Tonight I will surprise him with his favorite from the little take-out place we used to eat at when we were dating. The surprise of seeing me and the nostalgia of times when the love between us was palpable will be enough to pull us out of this funk we are in.

The day slips by and it's finally time to give Jake his tablet so I can have a few moments to get ready. In the quiet sanctuary of the bathroom, I stood before the mirror, looking over myself. My hair, usually up in a messy bun, is now down and straight. I never noticed how long it got. As I rummaged through my makeup bag, my fingers brushed against a forgotten relic – a vibrant shade of red lipstick that hadn't seen the light of day in what felt like ages. Intrigued by the sudden impulse, I uncapped the tube and swept the rich color across my lips. The mirror reflected a version of myself I hadn't encountered in years, a bold and daring echo from the past. But as I gazed at my reflection, an unexpected chill crept down my spine. In an instant, my reflection changes and she is standing behind me, her lips pressed to my ear as her hand runs up my throat. My mouth opens in shock, my chest aching for a breath I can't take, as she trails her tongue up my earlobe. The sensation sent shivers down my spine.

This isn't real
This isn't real.

The knock on the door forces me to open my eyes to the empty room I'm in. Just like that, she's gone again and I'm left breathless. My fingers trace the path she made up my throat with her bloody hands as I collect myself in front of the mirror. Another knock at the front door is the final push I need for my feet to start moving. Letting the sitter in, I explain that I shouldn't be more than a couple of hours, as I put the lipstick in my purse. Kissing Jake on the head, I grab my keys and walk out the door.

The engine hummed softly as I navigated through the city streets, the familiar scent of takeout wafting through the car. I turned up the radio, hoping the upbeat tunes would drown out the chaotic symphony of thoughts in my mind. Heat floods my ear, and my core, as I try not to remember her touch.

She showed up again.
She touched me.

Despite the blaring music, she still lingered in my thoughts, a persistent melody that refused to be silenced. As I drove, an unsettling notion took root – a fear that I was falling in love with the daydream version of myself. That bold, unapologetic woman felt like a manifestation of my own insanity in human form. Can you fall in love with a daydream? If I embrace her will I be embracing my own descent into madness? What is wrong with me?

I pushed the disconcerting thoughts to the recesses of my mind, focusing on the task at hand. A sliver of hope filled my chest as I glanced at the bag of food, a reminder of my attempt at fixing my marriage. Every couple goes through this, a period of becoming so comfortable in marriage that you forget to fan the flame.

Arriving at the office building, I turned off the car and took a deep breath. Reaching into my purse I pull out the tube of lipstick to touch up before I get out of the car. Walking into the building I stopped at the desk to sign in, the security guard at the front desk looked up, a friendly smile creasing his face. "That smells amazing! Lucky guy getting that for dinner."

I return the smile, trying to mask my nerves. "Thanks, he's been working late a lot lately. Thought I'd bring him a little treat."

The elevator ride was a slow ascent, each floor adding weight to the anticipation that clung to me like a heavy shroud. When the doors opened, the office floor lay quiet, an eerie contrast to the bustling workday it usually embodied. The secretary's desk sat vacant, and a hush settled over the space. The emptiness was deafening until the distant sound of voices broke the silence. I tiptoed toward Mark's office, heart pounding with each step. I hope he sees this for what it is, an attempt to mend whatever is broken.

"That's it, swallow it." A familiar voice whispers as I come closer to Mark's office.

My steps slow down and my enthusiasm seeps out of my pores. When I finally reach his office I see Mark's head tilted back, his face twisted with pleasure, oblivious to the spectator standing just beyond his line of sight. The food nearly slipped from my grasp, but I held on, my eyes locked in amazement at the betrayal laid bare before me. A tidal wave of rage surged within me, a torrent that seemed to originate from the deepest recesses of my chest. The quiet fury, once restrained, now roared to life, a fire that threatened to consume everything in its path.

As I stood there, hidden in the shadows, witnessing the intimate betrayal unfold before me, the anger built like a storm gathering strength. It was a primal force, coursing through my veins, seeking release. At that moment, my every fiber screamed for justice, for retribution against the unraveling tapestry of our marriage. Yet, I remained a silent specter, simmering with a rage that danced on the precipice of eruption.

Suddenly, I see her, not the woman swallowing my husband's unimpressive cock, but the woman that has taken my sanity hostage. The woman who sets me on fire with lust and longing. She stands there behind Mark, in all her gore-soaked beauty staring right at me.

Not yet.

Those words infiltrate my thoughts, settling on my skin like a warm blanket. Retreating silently, I rushed from the office, the weight of the truth echoing in my footsteps. The car door slammed shut, and I sat in the driver's seat, hands trembling on the wheel. Trembling, not with sadness, but with a rage that filled me to the brim of my being. Resting my head against the headrest I close my eyes for a moment, each deep breath aching in my chest.

Then a soft touch, a whisper on my skin as I open my eyes and see her. From the passenger seat, she is leaning across the console, her hand tilting my chin to her, softly. Her eyes bore into my soul, and my mind flashed with images. Images of Mark looking down with lust at the whore between his legs, as I stand behind him. Reaching up I wrench his head back by his hair and slit his throat with a letter opener. The spray of blood from his neck is a glorious sight as I bathe in it to the sounds of his whore's screams.

    She, my beautiful madness, leans closer to me waiting for me to take the plunge. As our lips meet in a passionate embrace, the lines between reality and fantasy blur into a kaleidoscope of chaos. The kiss, a desperate surrender to the intoxicating insanity within, leaves me breathless.

    Emerging from the kiss, a chilling calm settled over me, revealing a sinister plan taking root in the recesses of my mind.

    She's lost it.

Chapter Four

In the days following the gut-wrenching revelation of Mark's infidelity, I navigated the charade of a crumbling marriage with a practiced mask. Behind the veneer of a dutiful wife, my anger smoldered like an ember waiting to ignite. As Mark basked in his obliviousness, I secretly forged my own plans – a Valentine's Day surprise he wouldn't soon forget.

The canvas for my revenge unfolded within the confines of the she shed, a haven that would soon transform into a chamber of retribution. With a determination fueled by the simmering rage within, I meticulously soundproofed every inch, ensuring that the echoes of my retaliation would remain confined within its walls.

Layers of insulation, heavy curtains, and acoustic panels adorned the space. I immersed myself in the project while Jake played right outside the doors of the shed. Like all the hobbies before I researched everything I needed for this plan. The she shed, once a sanctuary of solace and naughty memories, morphed into a cocoon of secrets and calculated vengeance. I used the money from the savings account we use for Christmas. Mark never keeps track of that one and the amount we had saved up was more than enough to get everything I needed.

As I put the finishing touches on the soundproofed sanctuary of the she shed, Jake played in the dirt, his laughter a balm to the turmoil within. If anyone should ever find out what will happen here, they won't place blame on Mark.

People, ever ready to label a woman unraveling, would chalk it up to the cliché of motherhood-induced insanity or untreated postpartum. Perhaps they were right, or perhaps they were blind to the real source of my turmoil. Motherhood, in its chaotic beauty, brought me joy.

It was not the culprit but rather the refuge from the storm unleashed by the betrayal I witnessed. If insanity gripped me, it was not the result of bringing life into this world but the consequence of witnessing the death of trust and love in my marriage. Blame may be laid at many doors, but the truth echoed in the hollow chambers of my soundproofed refuge – my descent into madness found its roots not in the cradle of motherhood but in the shattered vows of matrimony.

Closing the creaky doors of the shed, a sense of both nervous anticipation and newfound liberation stirred within me. The impending revenge plan loomed on the horizon, but for now, I turned my attention to Jake, lost in the wonder of playing with his toy dump truck in the mud. Seizing the opportunity to escape the mounting chaos in my mind, I plopped down beside him, commandeering a toy truck of my own. As we engaged in our miniature construction escapade, the weight of impending uncertainties post-revenge started to creep in. What will happen to Jake if I have to go away? What happens if I don't have to go away? I will need to get a job. Who will watch Jake while I'm gone?

The thoughts raced, gaining momentum until Jake flashed me a mischievous smile, embracing me with tiny, mud-covered hands. At that moment, I felt a reassurance that somehow, we'd figure it out. Just as I was about to drown in the sea of unknowns, Jake took his toy dump truck, tipped it, and gleefully exclaimed, "I dump on you!"

Laughter erupted as dirt cascaded over me, and suddenly, the gravity of the situation seemed to lift. In the midst of the mud, chaos, and uncertainty, I found unexpected joy, and all I could do was laugh along with Jake, grateful for the simple hilarity of the moment. We stayed outside till the sun started to go down and when I crawled into bed later that night I slept peacefully knowing everything would be ok.

The days slipped away, each passing moment adding a layer to the intricate tapestry of my revenge. Mark remained oblivious to the storm gathering beneath the surface, and as Valentine's Day approached, my outward demeanor masked the fury that raged within every time I looked at him. Until, a few days before Valentine's Day, the dinner table became a battlefield, the air thick with tension as Mark was actually home for dinner. What started out as a nice family dinner at the table ended in the final push I needed to commit to the plans I had laid out.

Jake, in his innocent excitement, spilled his drink, the liquid drenching Mark's food and lap, setting off a powder keg of frustration. Mark's eyes flared with irritation as he reprimanded Jake for his clumsiness, demanding that he learn some semblance of table manners.

"You need to teach him, Emily," Mark spat, his frustration pouring out. "And get your head out of the books or whatever else has your attention these days. I work all day, and all I want is to come home to a nice meal! Now I'm fucking soaked."

Defending Jake, I interjected, "Maybe if you were home more, you'd know that he always has my attention. Also, if you would let me give him a sippy cup this wouldn't happen."

Mark's face darkened with anger. "I told you he is too old for that shit. If you don't teach him now he's never going to learn."

Fighting the urge to unleash the rage simmering under my skin, I bit my tongue and asked, "Are you even happy here with us? You're never home lately and now you lash out against Jake, who in case you forgot is fucking three years old Mark. What happened to you? What changed that turned you into such a fucking asshole" I ask the question but I know what changed. The memory of that night in his office flashes across my mind as I get up to grab a dish towel to clean up the mess.

His response cut like a knife. "What changed is that along with the extra 30 pounds to your ass, you also added the fact that you're a nagging bitch now." With that, Mark slammed his plate into the sink beside me, the loud clang reverberating through the tense silence.

"Fuck you, you're pathetic. Yelling at a three-year-old." I mutter under my breath before I feel his hands on me. Jerking me around to face him, his hand wraps around my throat, pushing me into the counter till my back bends. My body shakes involuntarily although I stare straight into his eyes.

"You said you would never do this in front of Jake," I whisper through the hateful tears streaming down my face. Memories of before that I'd locked away flooded the room. He smiles thinking I'm still the weak woman who will cry and beg him to stop. Pushing my face roughly enough to hit my head on the cabinet he steps away from me. Looking at me with disgust he huffs shaking his head.

"I'm going to shower," he announced curtly, leaving the shattered remnants of our dinner behind, the turmoil of the evening lingering like an unspoken specter in the dimly lit kitchen.

Letting out the breath I was holding, I turned away from Jake's view. Gripping the counter I stare out the window above the sink as the she shed, now a fortress of retribution, stood ready to unveil the crescendo of my carefully orchestrated retaliation. As the clock ticked relentlessly toward the designated day of reckoning, I couldn't help but revel in the impending catharsis, a twisted form of closure that awaited us both.

Chapter Five

The morning after the explosive dinner confrontation felt like the aftermath of a storm. I woke to an empty bed, Mark's side untouched. A note lay on the bedside table, a feeble apology scrawled across the paper.

"Sorry about last night. Work's been hell. I'll make it up to Jake and you tonight. Promise."

As I read the note, the words held a feeble attempt at reconciliation, a promise to make amends for the previous night's outburst. Yet, the hollow apology fell on deaf ears. The anger he directed at Jake during dinner had breached an unspoken barrier, and there was no coming back from that. The look on Jake's face is burned in my memory along with the lasting images of his infidelity. He could write a book of promises and sweet words and I would rip out every page and wipe my ass with each one.

The thought has me smiling as I make my way to the bathroom. I open the cabinet to grab the small box from the back. The box that is usually filled with tampons, something Mark wouldn't go digging through, is now filled with a plastic bag that makes me gag just looking at it. I know if I opened this bag I would be hugging the toilet, the smell unbearable. The sides of the gallon-sized plastic bag streaked with a putrid brown sludge. The collection of lumpy shit is finally enough for what I have planned. Losing the battle of trying not to gag, I place the bag back in the box and push it back into its place in the cabinet.

Even though I didn't open the bag the urge to wash my hands was too strong to ignore.
As I stared into the mirror, she stared back, through my eyes. The change was palpable, a subtle yet undeniable shift in my perception of the world. The burdens that once weighed me down evaporated, replaced by an unsettling sense of weightlessness. I

felt like a puppet guided by an unseen force, my liberation laced with a sinister edge. A knowing smile twisted my lips as I acknowledged the possession that had taken root within. The impending revenge was so close I could feel it, and I was both puppet and puppeteer in this macabre dance of retribution.

Thoughts of his weak apology flicker in my mind and I laugh with my reflection. Stopping only to contemplate the notion of forgiveness, wondering if a "normal" wife would accept the note as truth. I found myself questioning the very essence of normalcy. Was it the idyllic scenes painted by television and movies, where love always conquered and forgiveness flowed effortlessly?

In my opinion, *normal* was not cheating on your wife and lashing out at your son. Reality seemed a stark contrast to the curated narratives of fiction, where happy endings were neatly packaged. The note remained just that – a note, unable to fix what has always been broken. The shards no longer cutting my fingers as I try to hold together the pieces.

With Valentine's Day tomorrow, a palpable sense of purpose guided my steps as I finished getting ready and packed Jake into the car for a hasty run to the store. Navigating the aisles, my cart now held two heart-shaped boxes of Valentine's chocolates, a bag of mulch, and a garden spade – seemingly innocent items that concealed the darker motives stirring within. The last thing before heading to checkout was a stop at the toy aisle so Jake could pick a few new toy cars to add to his collection. The act of letting him pick them out felt motivated by a small shred of guilt. A small trade being made unknowingly to him, a few toy cars to replace the fact that I'll be murdering his father.

At the checkout, an old lady with a warm smile observed Jake in the cart and couldn't resist striking up a conversation.

"Oh, what a cutie you have there," she remarked, her eyes twinkling.

I returned her smile, gratitude masking my underlying irritation. "Thank you. We're just picking up some last-minute things for Valentine's Day and maybe a little gardening project."

The old lady's eyes sparkled with curiosity. "Gardening, how lovely! Is this little one going to help Mommy with the garden?"

I chuckled, a bittersweet warmth enveloping my response. "Oh, absolutely. He's my little gardening assistant."

As she looked into the cart, her gaze lingered on the items, and with a knowing smile, she said, "Well, it's wonderful to see families working together. Happy gardening, dear."

I bid her farewell with a grateful nod, concealing the truth beneath the facade. Jake wouldn't be around when I planted that garden; his night was already scheduled at the sitter's, an integral part of the calculated plan set to unfold in a few days.

Later that evening, Mark returned home early as promised, and I watched him engage with Jake. the charade of a loving father was overshadowed by the knowledge of his deceit. Over dinner, Mark continued his apologetic rhetoric, weaving promises of change and more time spent at home. I nodded, feigning hope, but the truth lingered beneath the surface – this was just another act in his ongoing charade. The evening played out in a delicate dance of deception, the romantic gestures falling flat against the backdrop of the things I had planned.

Once we put Jake to bed we both settled into our sides of the bed. The hanging expectation of intimacy was turning my stomach. I didn't want to touch him.

Mark's phone emitted a series of discreet buzzes, his attention immediately drawn to the screen. The dim glow of the device illuminated his face, momentarily casting shadows on his features. Apologizing for the intrusion with practiced ease, he explained it was work and excused himself to his office. I was thankful for the intrusion, but curious. Intrigued, I silently trailed behind, positioning myself just outside the door, curiosity and suspicion intertwining.

In the hushed sanctuary of his office, Mark's voice took on a different cadence as he spoke into the phone "You know better than to call me when I'm at home," he admonished in a low murmur, a flicker of annoyance betraying his attempt at composure.

"I know it's Valentine's Day. That's why I reserved the room, you will have me all day but at night, I have to go home to Emily. She'll get suspicious if I stay at work on Valentine's Day."

I wasn't surprised by the calculated balancing act between the two worlds he had going on. "Don't forget the strap on this time. I'll let you fuck my ass before I wreck yours." He laughs into the phone.

Returning to the room, my mind raced with a curious mix of surprise and detachment at how experimental he was with this woman. Mark was as vanilla as they come. A bemused laughter bubbled within me, but I quickly stifled it, not wanting to reveal my awareness. I lay down, feigning sleep as Mark re-entered the room. The bed creaked under his weight as he tried to initiate a more intimate connection, his hand reaching for my shoulder. The disgust I felt was unmeasurable at how easy it was for him to tell this woman to fuck him in the ass only to come back and try to deliver his usual poor performance with me. I don't think so.

Silence greeted his advances, and when my response remained absent, he sighed, "fucking figures," he muttered before rolling over. He settled into bed, and the room fell into a hushed stillness. Still trying not to laugh I lay there playing out the scenes to come.

I'll fuck him alright, but this time I won't be left unfulfilled.

Chapter Six

The morning of Valentine's Day unfolded with a twisted sense of anticipation. Mark, seemingly oblivious to the brewing shitstorm coming, kissed me with a half-hearted wish for a happy Valentine's Day, shrouded in an apology for another day spent at work. I knew he wasn't going to work. He had a rather eventful day planned with a strap on and I had things to do anyway. I had a stage to set.

Seizing the moment, I smiled and dropped a hint about a surprise awaiting him that evening. "Make sure you're not late," I teased, a veiled promise lingering in the air, leaving him intrigued. His surprise at my sudden change of demeanor flickered across his face, a momentary break in the facade. Genuine curiosity replaced his usual indifference and I was filled with a giddy sort of excitement. Before he could walk out the door, I embraced him and whispered in his ear, "I can't wait to fuck you." The words meaning different things for both of us. Kissing his ear before pulling away I almost laughed at how they left him visibly taken aback, a hint of pleasure dancing in his eyes. "I won't be late," he promised, and the unsuspecting satisfaction in his voice pleased me. He had no idea what was coming.

Jake, full of boundless energy, followed me as I ventured into the backyard. Armed with a garden spade, I began my project, digging hole after hole in the earth while stopping intermittently to engage in playful moments with him. Laughter echoed through the air as Jake's tiny hands joined mine in the soil, oblivious to the underlying motives that fueled my actions.

The day passed by in a blur of activities and before I knew it the sitter arrived – a kind woman who had once worked at Mark's office. She was older, a widow with a warmth that radiated genuine compassion. I knew she hadn't been part of Mark's affairs; she wasn't his type, and her commitment to her late husband was unwavering. Her willingness to help care for Jake on Valentine's Day, a day that undoubtedly stirred her own emotions, revealed a selflessness that touched me. Grateful for the distraction, she happily embraced the role of providing Mark and me with a night to ourselves. Her gentle demeanor hinted at a marriage that had weathered the tests of time, a stark contrast to the turbulent storm of emotions that defined my own relationship. In a fleeting moment, I found myself yearning for a different reality, one where my marriage mirrored the kind of enduring love that she had seemingly known. Her presence stirred a complex mix of emotions – admiration for the love she had experienced, envy for the life I imagined she had led, and a silent wish that circumstances could have unfolded differently for me.

The reality I faced was far from that ideal, a stark truth that I had grown tired of denying. I had spent years attempting to fit into societal expectations, seeking fulfillment through various hobbies, only to find emptiness in the pursuit of happiness. Now, at the precipice of revenge, I had embraced the chaos within, unapologetically accepting the cards dealt to me. The facade of people-pleasing and endless searching for fulfillment had come to an end. Kissing Jake goodbye, I watch from the window as she drives away.

Turning my attention to the heart-shaped boxes I placed on the counter, One box remained untouched, a testament to the illusions of a conventional life, while the other's contents met its demise in the trash. Placing the empty heart-shaped box on the counter I walked to the bathroom. I retrieved the hidden plastic bag containing the ingredients for my impending act of revenge. It was a strange liberation, a journey into the heart of my own madness, and I had never felt more alive.

Carrying the bag of sloppy shit I forced myself not to gag; The actions I'm about to take are truly unhinged. I put on the pair of blue gloves and swallow the disgust I feel rising. Holding my breath I open the bag and use a melon baller to scoop out small spheres of thick feces. The dark brown lump surprisingly malleable stays together as I shape it into small squares. Feeling lightheaded I put down the melon baller and ran to the living room, releasing the breath I was holding. The smell still lingering makes the bile rise in my throat. I may be crazy but shit is still shit. Forcing myself to woman up, the phrase making zero sense in this situation, I finished the task of placing several small squares of gooey rancid shit on a pan and then covering them with melted chocolate to place in the freezer.

I remind myself that the outdated appliance is immediately being replaced after this. Mark won't be here to object to me spending "unnecessary money" after tonight. With everything almost in place, I walk down the hall to get ready.

In the dim glow of the bedroom, I could feel myself move with deliberate grace, my reflection in the mirror revealing a transformation. I shed the costume of the dutiful wife, replacing it with an air of confident allure. The room hummed with anticipation as I put on the lace-trimmed lingerie set that left little to the imagination. The fabric clung to my curves like a second skin, a testament to the newfound liberation coursing through my veins. I accentuated the ensemble with a sheer black robe that billowed seductively with each step. The air crackled with a potent energy as I applied the deep red lipstick from before, a bold declaration of the simmering desires I intended to unleash. This time he will get to see it. Looking at myself in the small shreds of clothes I felt confident. Confident that I look good and confident that the small scraps will be easy to burn when I'm done.

    I recognize the mischievous glint in my eye, the excitement coursing through my veins, it's almost time.

Chapter Seven

The clock ticks away the moments, and I find myself nestled in the quiet cocoon of anticipation. The once-empty heart-shaped box, now harboring my grotesque creation, rests on the table before me, its cover a deep red reminiscent of blood—fitting, considering the horrors planned for tonight. The other heart-shaped box sits beside it, a colorful cover with flowers, the contents way more desirable than the other one. My hand covers my mouth in an attempt to not laugh. An outsider would not think this is comical, but fuck the outsiders

. It's easy for the world to cast judgment on the wreckage of our union, to speculate and moralize on matters they've never endured. Until one walks the jagged path of heartbreak and disillusionment, they remain blissfully ignorant, shielded from the searing pain of shattered dreams and the bitter taste of unfulfilled promises.

Many women endure their pain in silence, conditioned to bear disrespect with stoic grace. I was guilty of it myself. Society's expectations, like oppressive shadows, force us into a role where our suffering remains invisible, veiled behind the illusion of picture-perfect family moments and extravagant vacations. These women were taught to uphold a standard of unwavering strength and craft a narrative of happiness that conceals the emotional turmoil beneath. The cracks in their spirits are cleverly hidden amidst smiling Facebook pictures, and the opulence of their getaways becomes a glittering distraction from the truth. In between those photos they usually feel unappreciated and forced to play a role in a movie they thought was a romance; turns out it's some sick domestic thriller. At least in my case.

I'm not saying every woman in the world is in some domestic prison, a lot of women are lucky. But even the lucky ones have felt unappreciated at one point.

The echoes of Mark's car approaching quicken my pulse, and a thrill of excitement courses through my veins. Tonight, the carefully woven threads of my revenge will unravel, and the she shed will bear witness to it all. Clad in lace and veiled in a sheer black robe, I stand by the door, a vision of allure awaiting him. The door swings open, and Mark enters, his eyes widening with a mixture of shock and desire. "Well, hello. Look at you."

His instinct to draw me into his arms is met with a playful resistance. "Wait," I whisper, producing a silky blindfold.

"No fucking way." He laughs at the sight of the shred of silk in my hands.

"Well, you can't have this," I say as I untie the robe draped around me to reveal the lingerie undeath, "Until you put this on." The confidence I feel is fueled but the thoughts of his blood on my hands later.

The desire in his eyes is surprising to me, especially since I know he spent the day fucking his office whore. He must think he is the luckiest man in the world. He gets to have us both, a buffet of flesh, for Valentine's Day that he put minimal effort into deserving. I fight back the sneer that threatens to cross my lips. Huffing out a laugh of excitement he turns around and bends down so I can tie the blindfold on. The urge to tie it around his throat instead makes my fingers twitch.

Grabbing the heart-shaped boxes, I cradle them with one arm and grab his hand with the other. "Now, no peaking." I tease. As I lead him through the house and out the back door, his tentative steps are fueled by curiosity and the thrill of the unknown. The soft crunch of gravel beneath our feet marks our journey to the she shed. "Em, where the fuck are you taking me." He laughs, still excited.

As we step inside, I turn to close the door. The seal silences everything that is about to happen in this building. Standing in front of him I make slow work of undressing him. When I have him fully naked and slightly shivering, I realize at one time I admired him. Now he just looks pathetic.

Leading him, I push him till his back is flushed against the back wall. His body jolts at the sound of chains as I lift and start to secure one of his wrists. "Holy shit, wait, Em. I don't know about being tied up." The trace of fear in his voice makes me laugh.

"Aw, what's wrong? You scared?" I lean in and grab hold of his cock, His body reacts instantly.

"Whoah, what has gotten into you? OK, fuck it. Let's do it." He says convincingly to himself.

I finish securing both wrists and ankles to the back wall. It wasn't hard to set up, just a little drilling, and Voila! I stand back to admire my handiwork, Mark spread out for me.

Suddenly, my mind flashes with images of her, Mark's face twisted in agony as she torturously scalps him. Peeling the layer of skin and hair back to expose the white of his skull.

"Hello, what are you doing? If you leave me tied up here Em, I swear I'll fucking kill you." Mark's voice pulls me back and the fake smile I wore disappears. "Emily!" he barks as I walk slowly towards him.

When my hands lightly graze his chest he flinches. I lean into him and press my lips against his. I remember his kisses used to make me feel beautiful, loved, and wanted. Now as I deepen the kiss, our tongues engaged in a sensuous ballet, a bitter taste fills my mouth. Pulling back slightly, my words a breath on his lips, I whisper "I told you I was going to fuck you." Before biting down on his bottom lip.

The pouty flesh mingles with the copper taste of blood as I sink my teeth into it. I don't let go even when his screams fill my mouth along with his blood. The chains rattle with his urge to push me away. When I finally let go, I stand back spitting the wine dark fluid in his face.

From the corner of my eye, I see her, sitting on the table, feet swinging playfully. The same table Mark fucked me on so long ago. She bites down on her finger, watching with lust in her eyes, motivating me to put on a show for her the way she did for me.

Let the show begin.

Chapter Eight

In the subdued light of the shed, the once-mighty Mark is reduced to a pitiable spectacle—bound, broken, and teetering on the precipice of his own vulnerability. The chains that entwine him serve as a stark reminder of the tangles he wove within our once-harmonious existence.

"What the fuck! What the.." Mark's words cut off between crying and the fact that he's spitting blood. The scene is almost erotic to me and I clench my thighs trying to stop the heat pooling there, knowing she's watching.

"Unchain me now, this is over. What are you? Fucking stupid?" he spits again.

"This is just the beginning baby." My words cut through the air like a knife as he pulls on the chains.

"Get these fucking chains off of me!" he yells straining to free himself without success.

"No fair, she got to fuck you! In the ass actually. Why can't I? I think I've earned a little fun being the dutiful wife and all." As if time stood still he froze, no longer pulling on the chains.

"What did you say?" he asks but he heard me.

"I said let's play a game!" lacing my voice with amusement I grab the heart-shaped boxes. "I probably shouldn't have bit you, seeing as how I have some delicious treats for you. But you're just so irresistible I couldn't help it." Laughing I open the box with the flowers on the lid, With a malevolent grin, I pluck a seemingly innocent chocolate from the box and approach Mark, bound and vulnerable.

"Open wide, Mark," I command as I lift his blindfold. He squints against the light but eventually locks eyes with me. Fear and anger mingle in his expression as I lift the chocolate to his lips. "Come on, play nice." I tease, savoring the desperation in his eyes as he clamps his mouth shut. With a firm hand, I force him to open his mouth peeling away at his bloody lips. He chews reluctantly, tears streaming down his face, the sweetness a cruel echo of our once-promising beginning.

"The beginning always starts off sweet, right?" I mock, relishing the irony.

"What are you talking about? This isn't a game Emily, you fucking hurt me. Let me down now or I'll scream." He threatens between swallowing the chocolate.

"I hurt you? I hurt you." I play with the words for a moment before a hysterical laugh bursts from my chest. "That's fucking hilarious coming from you. Oh, and by the way, I don't know if you've noticed but this whole place is soundproof. Scream all you want." His head jerks back and forth finally taking in his surroundings. I watch the panic flush his skin as his chest starts to rise and fall quickly.

Walking back to the boxes I pull from the other box a slightly imperfectly shaped chocolate. The chocolate coating barely covered the smell.

"What is this? What the fuck have you..." he tries to finish but I push the chocolate into his mouth.

As he takes one chew, the charade crumbles; he gags, spitting it out with a horrified scream. His eyes bulged out of his skull like overripe grapes, ready to burst with the pressure of his gags. "What the fuck is that?" he finally asks.

"Well, seeing as how I've taken your shit for so long I thought it only fitting you have some of mine, baby." If the adrenaline wasn't coursing through my body like a freight train I probably would throw up right about now. The way he stares at me in disbelief, his lip curled up in disgust revealing the brown sewage caked across his teeth. He desperately tries to spit out the fecal matter that is no doubt coating his tongue. The thick paste gagging him again as he begins to vomit on the floor.

Jumping out of the way to avoid the splash I stand beside her at the table. Her head is thrown back in laughter and surprisingly I join her.

"How does that saying go?" I ask her, "Life is like a box of chocolates." I cackle as I lean into her.

"You fucking psycho bitch!" he yells at me and both of our expressions go sour. Suddenly she is no longer beside me, like a flash of light she is standing by him staring at him in amused disgust. Turning my back to him I look at the table of things laid out before me, the remnants of my fleeting hobbies. Picking up the camera I stalk over to him, pretending to get the lighting right but not being able to find the right shot.

"Remember when I tried photography? You didn't like that hobby either. Everything I took an interest in was a waste of time. Waste of money. I enjoyed it for a while though. I loved the scenic shots. Not that you would actually take us anywhere but when you did I loved taking shots of flowers and shit like that." I talk not caring if he's listening.

"Anyone ever tell you you're really not photogenic." Pretending to be frustrated as he watches me, confusion smeared across his face. "Oh, I know. I never really liked portraits. Maybe if there were some flowers in here." I tap my chin, feigning a thoughtful expression as I go back to the table. Placing the camera down, I pick up the straight razor. When I turn around the light shines on the blade and I hear the chains before I can even look at him.

"Fuck, wait. NO. Stop. Emily. Please. This has gone too far. We can talk about this." He pleads with me as I walk over to him, razor in hand.

"Talk? Let's talk about you getting your dick sucked at work." I say and he shakes his head in disbelief.

I lean into him, trailing the razor down his chest until it reaches his dick, and his whole body stills.

"I don't know what you heard, but that's a lie. I swear it. Fuck! Emily, please." He shakes as I get down on my knees in front of him. His dick inches from my face.

"Like this right, in your office. Tell me to swallow it like you told her Mark." I look up at him as his nostrils flare with each breath.

"Emily, please." He begs, tears flowing freely now.

"Answer me this question, if you get it right, I'll put the razor down," I say as he nods his head crying.

"Where were you today?" I ask and the look on his face is pained. He closes his eyes, heavy tears flowing down his cheeks as he takes shaky breaths. For a moment I think he's going to tell the truth. Opening his eyes, he looks down at me.

" I was at work, working for us. For our family! I was going to stop and get you flowers but I kept my promise and showed up on time. I didn't even risk the chance of being late." He shouts, which really wasn't smart. But he never really was a smart one.

"Wrong. Now I think I'll make my own flowers." Bringing the razor's edge to his dick I place the blade in the tiny hole at the tip of his dick before I slice slowly, deeply up the shaft. The razor is sharp slicing through the veiny flesh inches away from the base. I continue to slice thick ribbons that way, wanting to be able to arrange the meat like a blooming flower. The agonizing screams coming from his body fill the space and I silently thank myself for soundproofing the building.

I squint in concentration as I try to manipulate the flesh how I want it but it just isn't working. I stand back accessing my work. " I just can't get the petals to fold right. It's giving weeping willow instead of pink lily. Not even camera worthy." I say as I head back to the table dropping the razor.

"Oh well, wouldn't be the first time your dick disappoints me." Snorting a laugh as I turn around. To my continued disappointment I see his head hanging, body twitching and anger floods my senses. Walking over, I pull his head up, as he groans. The piece of shit passed out.

"Well, you really are no fun, you know that Mark?" I huff trying to slap him awake, pinch him, poke him. Nothing works. I guess I'll just have to wait till he wakes up. Hopping up on the table, I wait. Bored already, I look down at the assortment of things on the table. When my eyes land on the crocheting needles a new sense of excitement has me jumping off the table.

"Perfect." I grab the razor again and make my way back to Mark's limp body. Beginning at his ribs, just under his armpit, I pull the skin with one hand and carefully slice down. Peeling the skin in thin skinny layers, I'm careful not to cut my own fingers as his body twitches. Laying the thin strips across my lap as I go, I work meticulously to get the perfect strips of flesh. The amount of blood pooling under him is almost too much, this fucker might just bleed out before I'm done. Finishing the task of skinning him I pick up the crochet needles.

Not long after, he takes in a gasp of air like he is coming from underwater. As his eyes snap open, pain etches across his features, he looks at me with pleading eyes.

"Emily, please, I'll change. I'll be better," he implores, the words barely escaping the agony that grips him. I ignore him, focused on the slippery shreds in my hands.

The admission of his infidelity spills out, staining the air with the weight of betrayal. "I was with her today, but you know that already. I'm fucking sorry. Please. Just let me go. I want our family back." he confesses, the admission hanging heavy in the tense silence. Yet, my focus remains steadfast on the rhythmic dance of crochet needles in my hands.

"I don't care, Mark," I respond, my tone devoid of emotion. The gravity of his pleas and confessions holds no sway over my determination. As he begs for release, I continue my stitching but fail to keep a hold of the wet strips of flesh.

"I didn't stick with crocheting very long either, did I?" I say giving up on the skin scarf I was attempting to make.

"Em, baby, please. I'm going to die here. Think about Jake. Please." He really is trying to pull out all the stops.

"Oh, you are definitely going to die here tonight. Which, in my opinion, is the best thing I could do for Jake. I don't want him becoming the type of man you are." I say shaking my head.

"You loved me once. You still love me Em. I know you do." He yells becoming desperate.

Walking closer, I embrace him, laying my head on his shoulder. My hands are at his sides as he hisses in pain.

"I did. I was madly in love with you Mark." Pulling away from him, my robe sticks to the sticky exposed red flesh from where I skinned him. I make a trail of kisses down his extended arm to his shackled hand.

"I used to wonder how these hands, the hands that used to touch me so tenderly, could also cause me so much pain. The times you wrapped them around my throat until I saw stars. The crazy thing is I longed for them to touch me even after all of that. I wanted you to caress me, show me the affection from before all the bullshit." The tears that sting my eyes surprise me.

"I'm sorry. I fucked up. I know that now." His words mean nothing because I've heard the same thing before over and over again. His fingers are cold as they reach to touch my face as I place a small kiss on his open palm. I lean into them letting him caress the side of my cheek.

"I promise. Just let me go." His eyes look weak but even hooded with pain I can still see the lies lingering in them. Suddenly, I feel the heat of her embrace on my back as she moves my hair from my shoulder. Placing soft kisses up my neck while her other arm snaked under mine to caress my breast. I lean back, eyes rolling with lust as she sucks and nips at my neck, her finger kneading the peak of my breast. As she continues to embrace me she softly guides my arm to the butcher saw hanging on the nail on the wall.

Chapter Nine

Her fingers laced with mine as I grabbed the butcher saw, Mark's curses and screams sounded distant as I'm lost in the ecstasy of it all. With one hand she helps me saw into the skin of Mark's wrist. The other hand pulling the panties of my lingerie aside. Leaning into her touch I saw through muscle, reaching the tough bone as she slides her fingers inside me. With each stroke of the saw, she pumps her fingers into me, her thumb circling my clit. Mark's agonizing screams are a distant melody as I work through the bone until finally, the hand falls to the floor in a puddle of blood.

Bending down she picks up the hand forcing me to the table with a frenzied need. The same table Mark fucked me on so long ago is where she now has me leaned back, exposing my sex to the cold air of the shed. The chill doesn't affect me as the heat of her touch floods all of my senses. She kisses me while trailing Mark's fingers down my neck. She pulls back as she gently moves his hand down my cheek lightly grazing my nipples with his bloody fingertips. I shake with the sensation of his hands finally touching in the way I've longed for. Bloody trails mark the path she made to my dripping cunt, she molds her hand to his as she places his fingers with hers into me and I gasp at the sensation.

    She guides Mark's cold fingers to reach the spot that makes me see stars. Pumping their fingers inside me, she thrusts her hips, kissing me deeply as I reach my orgasm, shaking everything off the table with my release. I feel her smile on my lips as I come down from the high of my orgasm. She throws the lifeless hand over her shoulder and I can't help but laugh.

    Helping me down from the table, I look over to Mark who hangs by one arm, barely alive. My feet almost slip in the blood that coats the floor as I make my way over to him, butcher saw in hand. When he weakly pulls his eyes up to meet mine, I bend down so he can hear me.

"I decided to take up gardening. I hope you don't mind." Head hanging, trails of blood and saliva flow freely from his mouth he tries to mutter something but I guess it doesn't really matter.

I spend the next four hours sawing through his body parts. I think he died halfway through his thigh but I'm not sure. Each chunk of flesh is small enough to bury in the predetermined holes outside.

By the time I have everything cleaned up and buried the sky looks like a bruise, deep purple fading into blue. I grab the box of chocolates, the one with the flowers on it, and reach for her hand. As our fingers intertwine, a delicate dance of vulnerability and connection unfolds. Her gaze meets mine with a warmth that transcends words, a silent proclamation of love that echoes in the shared silence between us.

In that moment, enveloped by the serenity of the evening, I feel an unfamiliar warmth coursing through my veins. For the first time in a long while, I am wanted, and the realization washes over me like a soothing tide. The depth of her gaze reflects a reservoir of emotions, and in that shared look, I discover an unexpected haven for my battered heart. I am happy, I finally allowed myself to surrender to the enchanting rhythm of affection that has blossomed between us. The act of embracing her, my sweet insanity, I find solace—a refuge from the storms that have raged within me for far too long.

As we sit on the back porch, The box of chocolates rests between us, a testament to the newfound tenderness that has blossomed in the wake of my tumultuous journey. In the quiet company of my sweet insanity whose hand I still hold, the promise of the sun on the horizon mirrors the awakening of my heart to the possibilities that lie ahead.

They will she lost it, but I found it. My sweet Insanity.

The End.

Printed in Great Britain
by Amazon